Cinderella's
Magical Wheelchair
An Empowering Fairy Tale

by Jewel Kats

Illustrated by Richa Kinra

From the Growing With Love Series

Loving Healing Press

Cinderella's Magical Wheelchair : An Empowering Fairy Tale
Illustrated by Richa Kinra

From the Growing With Love Series

Author's site www.JewelKats.com

Library of Congress Cataloging-in-Publication Data

Kats, Jewel, 1978-

Cinderella's magical wheelchair : an empowering fairy tale / by Jewel Kats ; illustrated by Richa Kinra.

ISBN 978-1-61599-112-9 (pbk. : alk. paper) – ISBN 978-1-61599-113-6 (hardcover : alk. paper)

[1. Self-realization – Fiction. 2. People with disabilities – Fiction. 3. Stepfamilies – Fiction. 4. Princes – Fiction. 5. Magic – Fiction. 6. Fairy tales.] I. Kinra, Richa, ill. II. Title.

PZ7.K157445Cin 2011

[E] – dc23

2011028455

Distributed by Ingram Book Group (USA), Bertrams Books (UK)

Published by

Loving Healing Press Inc.   www.LHPress.com
5145 Pontiac Trail   info@LHPress.com
Ann Arbor, MI 48105

Tollfree USA/CAN: 888-761-6268
London, UK: 44-20-331-81304

LOVING
HEALING
PRESS

For any child
who's faced an illness,
accident or injury.

In a Kingdom far, far away lives Cinderella. One summer evening, she's called while perfuming Stepmother's gym socks. Cinderella wheels into the kitchen super quick. Everyone is already seated around the oak dinner table.

"Hurry up, slowpoke!" Stepmother snaps. She drums her fingers. "I have important news to share."

"What is it, Mother?" the twins singsong.

Stepmother smirks. "The King is ill. He wants to see his only son married. He's hosting a costume party for the Prince to meet all interested women. And my girls are *interested*, alright!"

"How awesome!" the twins shout. They give each other high-fives.

"Will I be going?" Cinderella pipes up, twisting her hands nervously.

"You're kidding, right?" the elder-by-a-minute twin sneers.

"No, I'm not," Cinderella answers quietly. "I'd like to attend."

Both stepsisters lock their heavily made-up eyes. Together, they release a loud snort.

"I'm afraid we're talking about a royal costume party – not a charity ball," the younger twin says. "Wake up, Cinderella. Wheelchair-mobile Princesses don't exist."

Cinderella's cherry cheeks heat up.

"Now, now," Stepmother interjects, "there's no need to be rude. It's not like she's some threat."

Stepmother glares hard at Cinderella. "You enjoy jewelry-making in your spare time, correct?"

Cinderella nods. "Yes, ma'am."

"Well, then, I'll let you tag along if you manage to create stunning jewelry for the twins." Stepmother sticks out her bony hand. "Deal?"

"You can count on me," Cinderella says, sealing the agreement with a handshake.

The next week passes by in a whiz. During the daytime, Cinderella zips through her usual chores. After the sun sets, her storage room turns into a wild fashion house.

"Glue more garnets onto my hair clip!" one twin demands.

"I want sparkling pearls. NOW. Remake this necklace at once!" the other orders.

Once everyone is asleep, Cinderella stitches her butterfly costume in secret night after night. She also works on another surprise.

Finally, the big day arrives. Stepmother hires makeup masters and hotshot celebrity hairstylists for her daughters. As usual, Cinderella is ignored. She relies on her own skills to jazz herself up. Cinderella wheels out of her storage room quite pleased with her look.

The jaws of the twins drop. Their stomachs turn with vomit.

"Do you think you're a wonder of nature now?" the elder twin taunts.

"You'll never even walk – let alone dance with the Prince!" the younger twin states.

Ruthlessly, they claw at the butterfly wings of Cinderella's costume.

"Please stop!" Cinderella cries.

Stepmother rushes to the scene. She, too, is taken aback by Cinderella's beauty.

"Don't worry, girls," Stepmother says. "I'll take care of the situation." She runs into Cinderella's storage room and returns with a sharp jewelry tool.

Stepmother glares at Cinderella. "As far as I'm concerned, you're not going anywhere!" With that said, she punctures Cinderella's wheelchair tire.

Stepmother and her daughters laugh, and leave for the royal costume party arm-in-arm.

"What about our 'deal'?" Cinderella sobs.

"Don't cry," an unfamiliar voice says.

Cinderella looks up. "Who are you?"

"My name is Monique, and I'm a student fairy godmother from Enchantment University. I'm here to help you get to the royal costume party."

Cinderella blinks.

"Have some faith," Monique says, shaking her dreadlocks. "First, we need to get your outfit in order. I'm thinking Old Mother Hubbard. I'm thinking Little Bo Peep – "

Cinderella frowns. "I worked hard on the costume I designed."

"Gotcha," Monique says, tapping Cinderella's shoulder with a magic wand. Immediately, a set of tiny ballerinas appear. They twirl about while re-stitching her torn costume.

Cinderella blinks twice.

"Next, I need to get you out of here," Monique announces.

Right then, Cinderella and Monique land outside on the driveway. Only, they're seated in an out-of-service Wheel Trans bus.

"Whoops!" Monique says. "I must've dozed off during that Transportation and Magic class. Let's try again."

Monique squeezes her eyes shut. Cinderella and her wobbly wheelchair shoot up lightening fast. Fireworks sound. Her wheelchair transforms. It's no longer damaged, but rather futuristic. Cinderella's wheelchair sports twenty-four karat gold rims, a blinking control panel and mighty airplane wings.

"This magic isn't going to last forever," Monique shouts from down below. "*Everything* will slip back at midnight. Until then, have fun!"

"Thank you!" Cinderella says, blowing a goodbye kiss from the stars. In seconds, she's flying to the palace.

Meanwhile, the Prince sits alone. He pokes at the stinky blue cheese on his plate. His eyes wander to a banquet window, and the most extraordinary sight catches his attention. The Prince sees a costume-clad woman flying on a wheelchair. She truly looks like a gorgeous butterfly. He scoots out to get a better look.

"You've come too late, Miss," a security guard huffs at the gate.

The Prince hurries. Then, he sees her.

"Let her in, Stan," the Prince orders.

Cinderella recognizes his famous face in a snap.

"Are you flying in from another party?" the Prince asks.

Cinderella smiles shyly. "No, I haven't gone out in ages."

The Prince raises an eyebrow. "Really? Please tell me more around the palace garden."

Cinderella and the Prince talk about everything under the moon.

She hands him an envelope. "I made a get-well-soon card for the King. I hope my surprise helps him feel better."

The Prince bites his lip. "You're the only woman today who's stopped to think of my dad. That means a lot to me."

Cinderella holds the Prince's hand. "I know how much it hurts to see a parent get sick. Both of my folks passed away from an illness."

"I'm sorry to hear that," the Prince says.

Cinderella smiles. "It's okay, I've learned to survive."

"You're a wonderful woman," the Prince says. "Would you honor me with a dance?"

"I, um," Cinderella says, staring at her sleeping legs. Then she remembers her magic wheelchair. "Let's go!"

Partygoers watch Cinderella and the Prince make their way to the dance floor. The King looks on, too. Cinderella starts bopping her head. Her seat rises. The tires of her wheelchair start bouncing with the beat.

The entire banquet hall is buzzing with ooohs and ahhhs. Cinderella's stepfamily scowls.

Cinderella moves away once a romantic tune takes over.

"Hey, why did you stop dancing?" the Prince asks.

Cinderella stares at the cold marble floor. "My magic wheelchair can't boogie to slow songs."

The Prince lifts her chin up. "We don't need any hocus-pocus to dance." He scoops Cinderella into his arms, and they sway to the music.

Kingdom clocks immediately sound with twelve loud chimes.

"It's time to leave!" Cinderella cries.

Her magic wheelchair gets into position.

"Put me down at once!" Cinderella orders.

The Prince does so, and she takes off.

He chases after her. "Wait up!" The Prince grabs onto Cinderella's hand, and pulls a lace glove from it.

In a flash, Cinderella and her magic wheelchair are gone.

Monique was right. The magic spell did break at midnight. Everything changed back just like that. Other changes happened, too. Cinderella woke up to see life for what it is. She moved out of her stepfamily's cruel nest. She now rents a cool wheelchair-accessible apartment in downtown. Cinderella kicked-off her own jewelry-making business as well. Success is of her own making.

One day, the Prince surprises Cinderella by showing up in her jewelry shop.

"I've been searching for you EVERYWHERE," the Prince says. "Why didn't you reply to my radio or TV ads?"

"Honestly," Cinderella answers, "I don't have a magic wheelchair. I didn't think you'd be interested in plain old me."

"How you get around ISN'T important," the Prince replies. "I like YOU because of YOU. We make a complete pair together."

The Prince pulls out her missing lace glove from his pocket.

Eventually, Cinderella and the Prince start planning their wedding. Cinderella decides to send out an invitation card to her stepfamily. In return, they mail a large gift box to the palace.

"What can be inside?" Cinderella asks the Prince.

She unties a pretty pink bow. Once opened, the box reveals a pair of Stepmother's yucky gym socks and a bottle of used perfume.

"Enjoy your wedding prezzie," Stepmother and the twins have scribbled onto a note.

Despite this, Cinderella and the Prince have a grand wedding. Newspaper and TV reporters from around the world cover the event. Life afterwards is peachy, too. The Prince makes sure the palace is wheelchair-accessible. Cinderella continues to work as a jewelry-maker. Together, they volunteer to help people in need. Clearly, Cinderella's stepsister was dead wrong – wheelchair-mobile Princesses DO exist!

About the Author

Jewel Kats, 32, is an award-winning writer. She's also one tough cookie. At the age of nine, Jewel endured a car accident. Her physical abilities altered forever. She spent weeks in the Hospital for Sick Children recovering, has survived eight leg surgeries, and currently walks with a cane. (Note: It's fashionally hand-painted!) Nothing stops Jewel. For six years, she penned a syndicated teen advice column for Scripps-Howard News Service and TorStar Syndication Services. Jewel has earned $20,000 in scholarships from Global Television Network and Harlequin Enterprises Ltd. She's penned three children's books, including: "Reena's Bollywood Dream" and "What Do You Use to Help Your Body?" This fairytale took her five years to write. It's just that special! Jewel is now working on a movie screenplay. She calls Toronto home.

Please visit her website at: www.jewelkats.com

About the Illustrator

Richa Kinra is the internationally published illustrator of several children's books, adult fiction books and spiritual poems. Her books include titles as *Fuzzball goes to the Mall, Emilie is...Princess for a day, Debra Meets Her Best Friend In Kindergarten, Annabelle's Secret, Reena's Bollywood Dream*, and others.

She lives in India with her family, and says she received a lot of encouragement from her parents and friends who saw her artistic talent.

Her hand painted works are primarily in watercolors, acrylic and oils, sometimes incorporating colored pencil, dry colors, pen & ink and/or collage.

What do you use to help your Body ?
by Jewel Kats
Illustrations by Richa Kinra

Juvenile Fiction : Social Issues - Special Needs

Maggie and Momma love going for walks. During every outing, Maggie learns about something new. Today's no different! Momma has arranged for Maggie to meet lots of people in her neighborhood. They all have different jobs. They all come from different cultures. They all use different things to help their bodies. Maggie doesn't just stop to chit-chat. Rather, she gets to the bottom of things. By asking the right question, she discovers how many people with disabilities use aids to help them out. Let's find out how they work, too!

- Children will learn that disabilities occur in every culture
- Parents and teachers can accurately explain how various disability aids work
- Children will realize that working with a disability is a possibility for some
- Therapists can use this book as a motivational tool for patients with disabilities
- Kids can satisfy their curiosity about disability aids in an unimposing manner

Paperback: $16.95   ISBN-13: 978-1-61599-082-5
Hardcover: $29.95   ISBN-13: 978-1-61599-096-2
Ask your local bookseller for this and other titles in the *Growing With Love Series*

www.LHPress.com/growing-with-love

Reena's Bollywood Dream
Jewel Kats

Reena wants to be a star… A Bollywood star. Unfortunately, her family won't stand for it. It doesn't help that Reena is only eight-years-old. However, a beacon of hope arrives in the form of Uncle Jessi. He's just emigrated from India to America, and is a welcome addition to her family household. Uncle Jessi and Reena share a special bond. Not only are they old pen pals, but he recognizes her desperation to become a Bollywood actress. One day, Uncle Jessi plans a secret surprise. He invites her to take part in a pretend acting game. Reena jumps at the chance. At first, she enjoys swinging her hips to Bollywood beats. She smiles brightly at his camera. However, halfway through her performance matters take an unexpected turn. The end results surprise both Reena and Uncle Jessi.

- Children will learn that sexual abuse is NEVER their fault.
- Parents and children will be given a launching pad to discuss the warning signs of "grooming."
- Children will come away knowing they have the power to say: "NO."
- Children will discover that sexual abuse can occur in any cultural group.
- Children can be assured that they will be believed when reporting inappropriate behavior.
- Therapists and parents can exhibit that sexual abuse isn't an off-limits topic.
- Child abuse survivors will come away knowing they are not alone.

Paperback: $15.95   ISBN-13: 978-1-61599-014-6
Hardcover: $29.95   ISBN-13: 978-1-61599-059-7
Ask your local bookseller for this and other titles in the *Growing With Love Series*

www.LHPress.com/growing-with-love

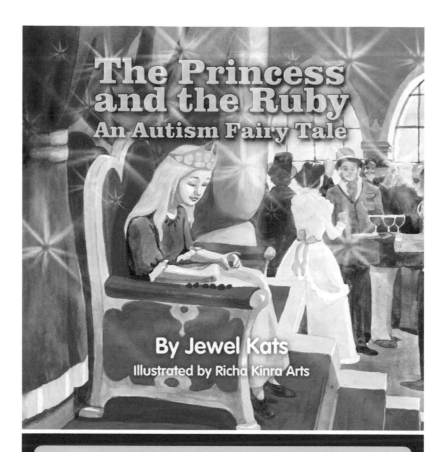

JUVENILE FICTION: SOCIAL ISSUES – SPECIAL NEEDS

A Mysterious Girl Puts the Future of a Kingdom in the Balance!

One icy-cold winter night, everything changes: a young girl shows up at the king and new queen's castle doorstep wearing little more than a purple jacket and carrying a black pouch. The king recognizes the mystery girl's identity as the long-lost princess without her uttering even a single word. However, the new queen refuses to believe the king's claims. In turn, a devious plan is hatched… and, the results are quite fitting!

- This new twist on Hans Christen Andersen's *The Princess and the Pea* is surely to be loved by all fairy tale enthusiasts.

- *The Princess and the Ruby: An Autism Fairy Tale* adds to much-needed age-appropriate literature for girls with Autism Spectrum Disorder.

- Both fun and education are cleverly weaved in this magical tale, teaching children to be comfortable in their own skin and to respect the differences of others.

Acclaim for *The Princess and the Ruby*:

"As someone who has a couple of friends with Autistic kids, I understand the challenges these families have. This modern day twist on *The Princess and the Pea* not only shows how others judge something they do not understand, but how someone with Autism can see, feel and do things one might not expect."
—V.S. Grenier, *Mom's Choice Silver Honoree* and award-winning author

"*The Princess and the Ruby* is a heartwarming narrative; a tale that beautifully depicts several unique characterizations of Autism Spectrum Disorder. Jewel Kats has refreshingly shed light upon a daily struggle to redefine 'normalized behaviors', in an admirable effort to gain societal acceptance and respect."
—Vanessa De Castro, Primary Residential Counselor with Autistic Youth

Paperback: $16.95   ISBN-13: 978-1-61599-175-4
eBook: $29.95   ISBN-13: 978-1-61599-176-1

Ask your local bookseller for this and other titles in the *Growing With Love Series*

www.LHPress.com/growing-with-love

CPSIA information can be obtained at www.ICGtesting.com
Printed in the USA
LVIW01n2150030615
441123LV00009B/57